Problems with a Python

by

Jeremy Strong

Illustrated by Scoular Anderson

You do not need to read this page –
just get on with the book!

First published in 1999 in Great Britain by
Barrington Stoke Ltd
www.barringtonstoke.co.uk

This edition published 2006

ISBN-10: 1-842993-80-1
ISBN-13: 978-1-84299-380-4

Printed in Great Britain by Bell & Bain Ltd

Meet The Author - Jeremy Strong

What is your favourite animal?
A cat
What is your favourite boy's name?
Magnus Pinchbottom
What is your favourite girl's name?
Wobbly Wendy
What is your favourite food?
Chicken Kiev (I love garlic)
What is your favourite music?
Soft
What is your favourite hobby?
Sleeping

Meet The Illustrator - Scoular Anderson

What is your favourite animal?
Humorous dogs
What is your favourite boy's name?
Orlando
What is your favourite girl's name?
Esmerelda
What is your favourite food?
Garlicky, tomatoey pasta
What is your favourite music?
Big orchestras
What is your favourite hobby?
Long walks

This is for everyone
who suffers from
an older sister ... or brother

Contents

Chapter 1
A Visitor

Adam pressed his nose against the glass tank.

"It doesn't look a very big snake," he told his friend.

Gary rolled his eyes.

"That's because she's curled up round herself," he said. "I'm telling you, she's over a

1

metre long. Anyhow, she's not meant to be *that* big."

"I thought pythons were huge."

"Not when they're small," Gary pointed out simply. "They have to be small first of all. This one is still a baby – well, a toddler at any rate."

Adam tapped the glass, but the snake didn't budge. "What do you feed it on?"

"She's not an 'it' and you won't need to feed her," answered Gary. "We're only going away for a week to stay with my Gran." He looked lovingly at the snake. "She won't need a meal for days. She ate a whole rat last night."

"Urrgh! That's revolting," said Adam.

"What do you expect pythons to eat? Jelly babies? Ice cream?"

Adam still looked rather put out, but he did ask his friend if the snake had a name.

Gary grinned. "Steak & Kidney."

"That's not a name!"

"Yes it is. Steak & Kidney. Get it?"

Adam shook his head and Gary rolled his eyes again.

"No, of course you don't. Steak & Kidney Pie ... python ... yeah?"

"Very clever," said Adam. "This name has nothing to do with the fact that your snake eats steak and kidney?"

Gary burst out laughing. "I never thought of that. That makes it even better."

Adam gave a pale smile. It was a bit amusing, although the rat probably had not found it funny at all.

Gary took the lid off the tank. He reached inside and pulled out the python. She dangled sleepily across his arms. Gary held her out and Adam took a step back.

"She's all slimy," he said.

"Don't be stupid. Snakes aren't slimy. That's just their scales shining."

"Yeah?"

"Yeah. Go on. You hold her."

Gary dumped the python into Adam's arms. He almost dropped her. He was not expecting her to weigh so much. Adam stood there, gritting his teeth, while the snake coiled around his left arm. The thick body was beautifully patterned with black, brown and gold markings. The thin, forked tongue darted in and out.

"She likes being stroked and having her belly tickled," Gary said.

"I am *not* going to tickle a snake's belly," snorted Adam. He couldn't think of anything more crazy.

"OK, but you will look after her while I'm away, won't you? You don't even have to get her out of the tank if you don't want to ... I mean, if you're *scared* ..."

Steak & Kidney slowly slithered up Adam's arm. Adam screwed up his face. The python pushed her hard, flat head beneath Adam's chin. She slid up Adam's cheek. The tongue began flickering again. Adam swallowed several times.

"I'm not scared," he croaked.

"That's all right then," smiled Gary. "I can see she likes you. She sticks her tongue in my ear too. If she tries to nibble your neck just keep very still."

"What!"

"Only joking," laughed Gary. He unwrapped the python from Adam's head. "Thanks for looking after her anyhow. I'll see you in a week."

Adam had both eyes fixed on Steak & Kidney, who was slowly settling back in the tank.

"Yeah, OK. Bye."

A few moments later the front door banged and Gary had gone. Adam was alone with one whole metre of Indian Python. He watched the snake as it curled up once again at the bottom of the tank.

A snake was not a very interesting pet. All she did was lie there. Adam threw himself onto his bed and stared at the ceiling. There must be something he could do with a python.

Chapter 2
Shock! Horror!

"How much longer are you going to be?"

Adam's big sister Emma banged angrily on the bathroom door. Emma was definitely Getting Ready For The Boyfriend. She stood outside with her arms full. She had shampoo and face masks. She had eyebrow tweezers and nail clippers. She had soap and bath foam and bubble mix. She had lipstick and eye-shadow.

"Just hurry up, will you? You've been in there hours and hours. Rob will be here any minute."

"I'm on the loo," said Adam. "You can't hurry that sort of thing."

Adam listened quietly as Emma stamped back to her room. He smiled to himself. He was not sitting on the loo. He was standing in the bath and carefully draping Steak & Kidney around the shower head.

Adam got out of the bath. He pulled the shower curtain so that the snake was hidden. From down below he heard a distant *bing-bong* of the door bell. Emma was back in a flash, hammering on the door.

"Let me in!" she squealed. "Rob's here! You've made me late. I haven't even washed my hair. I'm a wreck!"

Adam flushed the unused loo and opened the bathroom door.

"It's all yours," he said.

Emma pushed past him in a fury. "I'm going to kill you!" she hissed.

"Oh no, not again."

"Ha ha," sneered Emma.

She slammed the bathroom door and locked it. Adam went to his room and sat on his bed. He began counting quietly to himself.

"One, two, three, four, five, six ..."

"Aaaaargh! Eeek! Oh my God! Aaargh!"

The bathroom door shook with blows. The lock shot back. The door exploded open and out rushed Emma. She was clutching a towel.

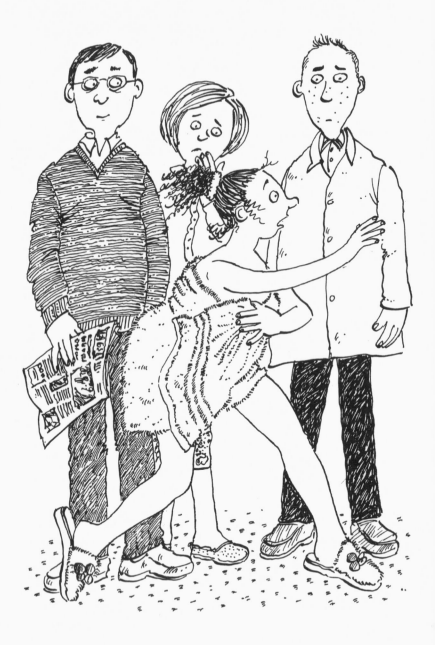

"Snake!" she yelled. "Snake in the shower!"

Emma fled down the stairs. Her astonished parents turned to look at her. An even more astonished boyfriend also stared at her.

"Wow," mumbled Rob, his eyes boggling. "Nice dress."

"There's a snake in the shower!" screamed Emma. "Aren't you going to save me?"

Mr and Mrs Laker looked from Emma to Rob and back to Emma. They were wondering what would happen next. Rob began to move towards the door. His spotty face had gone rather red and he nodded slowly. He was thinking.

"You did say a snake?" he asked.

"It was hissing at me from the shower head," squawked Emma. "Go on, go and catch it."

"Er, I'm not very good with snakes," said Rob.

Emma stopped trembling. She folded her arms and glared at her boyfriend.

"You're scared," she snapped.

"No, no," said Rob. "It's just that when I try to catch them they sort of slip out my hands – can't get a grip." He suddenly had a thought. "I can do tortoises. I caught one of those once."

Mr Laker hid a smile and went to the stairs.

"Go and get dressed Emma. It's only Gary's python. Adam's looking after her while Gary's on holiday. We thought you knew."

Emma stood there, a thundercloud on two legs.

"Nobody tells me *anything*. I might have known it would have something to do with my stupid little brother."

Mrs Laker put an arm round her daughter's shoulder.

"I expect Adam let her out by mistake. We did tell him to make sure she stayed in the tank."

"It's so embarrassing," muttered Emma, holding her towel closer. "I'll kill him."

Rob smiled at her. "I think you look nice," he said.

"Oh shut up!" snapped Emma.

"Right," said Rob, and he stared at the floor.

The room filled with an uncomfortable silence. Mrs Laker tried to keep up the small talk. She turned to Rob.

"Was it a big tortoise?" she asked politely. Rob began nodding again.

"It was about the size of a grapefruit," he said. "But that was with its head and legs pulled in. It was bigger when they stuck out."

"That must have been so scary," Emma said icily.

"Yeah," grinned Rob, completely missing her sarcasm. "They can bite, you know."

Mr Laker called down from the bathroom.

"All clear. The snake's back in the tank." He stood at the top of the stairs. "Adam says the snake must have escaped somehow."

Emma went nervously into the bathroom and shut the door once again.

Inside his bedroom Adam had his head stuck under his pillow. He was kicking his legs wildly. He hadn't laughed so much for weeks. So, what could he do next?

Chapter 3
Flies, Bees and False Teeth

Monday was a school day. Adam was still alive, in spite of what Emma had said, so he had to go to school. Sunday had been such a success that Adam had decided to take Steak & Kidney to school. He stuffed the sleeping snake into the bottom of his bag.

Adam thought his friends would be impressed if he turned up with a real python. His teacher, Mrs Batty, was always telling them

to bring in things that interested them. Only last week The Lovely Linda had taken in a piece of amber with a dead fly stuck inside it. She said the fly was millions of years old. Adam's friend Gary told her that he had a piece of soap at home with a moth stuck on it. He could bring that in. Lovely Linda told Gary he was stupid. Gary told The Lovely Linda that she was more stupid than he was. It was a high quality argument.

Adam agreed with Gary. He thought that The Lovely Linda was a pain in the neck. Just because she was very pretty she thought she was the bees' knees. Adam thought she was more like a bee's bottom. The Lovely Linda had a nasty sting. Adam wanted Steak & Kidney to be a big surprise for Linda. He couldn't wait to see the snake dangling round her neck. If he was lucky the python might even strangle her.

When Adam reached school there was great excitement. Some of the boys had been playing football. The ball had hit Mrs Batty on the back of her head and her false teeth had come shooting out of her mouth. They had landed somewhere in the school's little garden plot. Half the class were trampling about the garden, hunting for Mrs Batty's false teeth. Adam put his bag in the classroom and went off to join in the hunt.

"I never knew Mrs Batty had false teeth," he said to Martin Newgate.

"You don't know anything, full stop," muttered The Lovely Linda.

Adam scowled and kept quiet. After all, he had a dark secret hiding in the bottom of his bag. Lovely Linda would soon change her tune.

At last Mrs Batty's teeth were discovered, half-way up an apple tree. The teacher hurried back to class to give them a good wash. She popped them back into her mouth. After that she felt a lot better.

The whistle went and everyone began to troop into school. Adam grabbed his bag and sat down next to Martin.

"Guess what I've got in here," he whispered.

"How should I know?"

"A snake. It's Gary's. I'm looking after her for him."

Martin's eyes were boggling. "You haven't brought Gary's python to school?"

"Yeah. Look."

Adam reached into his bag. He pushed his hand right down to the very bottom. He felt all round with his fingers. The only thing down there that looked at all like a snake was a football sock. Adam pulled his hand from the bag. His face had turned white and he gazed at Martin. He was horrified.

"Oh dear," he groaned. "She's escaped."

The news spread rapidly. It was hissed from ear to ear in a series of undercover whispers. Mrs Batty raised her eyes from the register. She could tell something was going on, but what? Class 6B smiled back at her. Mrs Batty didn't question them. She had been teaching children for many years. She knew that if she kept quiet long enough they would soon give themselves away.

The class quickly divided into two camps. There was Adam's team – they firmly believed in the snake, even though none of them (except Adam) had seen it. Then there was Lovely Linda and the rebels. Lovely Linda sneered at him.

"You did *not* bring a python to school," she hissed. She sounded rather like a snake herself. She turned to her friends. "He's just trying to make himself look big."

"No I'm not!" Adam's face was a deep red.

The Lovely Linda laughed.

"Look at his ears! They're on fire!" Her laughter turned into a dark scowl. "That's how I know he's lying through his teeth."

"You're just jealous," Adam muttered.

"Jealous? Of you? Give me a break."

The Lovely Linda flashed her perfect teeth in a dazzling smile and swept away with her sniggering friends.

Even one or two of Adam's friends began to ask questions. "Where exactly is this snake, Adam?"

Adam groaned. If only he knew.

Chapter 4
A Monkey in the Hall

Mrs Batty lined everyone up at the classroom door for assembly. 6B trooped down the corridor and into the hall. A hundred and fifty other children were already sitting there and waiting. 6B sat down. Half of them began twisting this way and that. They were trying to spot the escaped snake.

Mr Twigg, the headteacher, began to talk. His sharp gaze scanned the children as he

spoke. What on earth were 6B doing? Their eyes were all over the place. They were looking everywhere except where they should be looking.

"6B! Have you got a problem?"

A slow chorus came rumbling back. "No, Mr Twigg."

"What have I just been saying to you? Tracey Grant, you answer."

Tracey swallowed as the whole school turned to look at her. Even Adam turned to look, and as he did he caught a very slight movement, high up on one wall of the hall.

Adam froze.

"Um," began Tracey. "You said 'Good morning everyone', Mr Twigg."

The rest of the school laughed.

"You haven't been listening, Tracey. Pay attention from now on. Everyone stand. We will now sing today's song."

Adam had his eyes glued on the wall bars at the far end of the hall. Steak & Kidney was folded around the very top bar, in full view of the whole school. Adam was about to nudge Martin but he stopped himself. It was better to keep quiet. If he told Martin, then Martin would tell Tracey and she would tell Sandeep and so on. Then the whole school would spot the snake and then – DISASTER!

Adam mumbled the words and kept his fingers crossed. He hoped that nobody would spot the snake so high up. Maybe after assembly he could sneak back and catch the python.

Assembly seemed to go on for hours. Adam tried not to look at the wall bars. Every so often, when he could not bear the strain any

longer, he took a quick peek. Steak & Kidney
didn't move. The snake seemed to be fast
asleep.

As soon as they were back in class Adam began to pester Mrs Batty.

"I really need to go," he whined.

"Cross your legs," she suggested.

"They are crossed, and I still need to go."

From behind him Adam heard The Lovely Linda pass some dark remark about potties. Several children burst out laughing. Mrs Batty turned on them.

"We would all like to hear the joke," she snapped. "Linda, maybe you would like to share it with everyone?"

Linda shook her head and kept quiet.

Mrs Batty sighed. "All right Adam, go to the toilet if you must."

Adam shot from his chair and raced from the classroom. He hurried down the corridor. He tip-toed past the secretary's office. He sneaked past Mr Twigg's shut door. He slipped into the hall and scanned the wall bars at the far end. Steak & Kidney was still there. The snake was festooning the top bar like a piece of leftover Christmas decoration.

Adam ran across the hall and began climbing. In a few moments he had reached the dozing snake. He gave a sigh of relief. At last he had the snake back, safe and sound.

"Come on," he said quietly. "Time to get you back into my bag. Come on."

Even as Adam spoke, the hall doors burst open. Twenty-eight six-year-olds came dancing in and began racing round in their vests and pants and little plimsolls.

The teeny-tots laughed and yelled at each other. Miss Raza, their teacher, walked in and began to shout instructions.

"Run round, everyone! Jump as high as you can! See if you can touch the ceiling!"

The infants leaped about like escaping baby rabbits, jumping and shouting. The noise woke Steak & Kidney. The python stirred. She blinked and began slowly to uncoil.

Adam hissed at the snake.

"Don't move! Stop it!"

But the snake calmly carried on. She began to slide along the bar.

"Come back!" whispered Adam, as loudly as he dared. "Come here, you stupid bit of sausage! Are you deaf?"

Adam edged after the snake as quietly as he could.

All at once one of the infants stopped, stared and pointed at the wall bars.

"A monkey! There's a monkey!"

Chapter 5
A Strange Boy

Everyone stopped. Then all the children began shouting. "Monkey! Monkey!"

Miss Raza hurried to the bottom of the wall bars and gazed upwards.

"Adam Laker – what on earth are you doing?" she demanded. "How long have you been up there?"

"I don't know," Adam answered lamely. He clung to the top bar.

"You don't know? Does Mrs Batty know you are up there?"

"No."

"Come down at once."

Adam slowly crept down the bars. Miss Raza was not very impressed with his behaviour. "What were you doing up there?"

Adam squeezed his eyes tight and tried desperately to think of an answer.

"Um ... hiding," he croaked.

"Hiding! What on earth from?"

"A – a spider," said Adam. "I'm scared of spiders. I saw one and I climbed up the wall bars to escape. Then you came in and I was afraid to come down again."

"You strange child," said Miss Raza, shaking her head.

"He's a monkey," shouted one little six-year-old.

"He's a baby," said one boy. "I'm not scared of spiders. Only babies are scared of spiders."

"And elephants," put in a small girl.

"Yes, and elephants."

"And whales too. Whales are scared of spiders."

"Don't be silly," said the boy crossly. "Whales are found in the sea and spiders are found on dry land," he said.

"I meant swimming spiders," insisted the girl.

She reminded Adam of The Lovely Linda, always getting in the last word.

Miss Raza took control.

"That's enough everyone. Adam, go back to your classroom at once. Mrs Batty will be wondering where you are. I shall talk to her at break time. I have never heard such a story. Go on, off you go."

Adam sighed and trudged back to the classroom. At least nobody had spotted Steak & Kidney. The snake had slipped away. But where had she gone? She could be anywhere. The minutes ticked away. Adam was churning inside. He expected screaming to start at any moment. But the school stayed strangely quiet.

Break-time arrived. Out on the playground two groups gathered. One group listened eagerly to Adam as he told them about the python on the wall bars. The other group giggled and sniggered. The Lovely Linda poured scorn on the very idea of there being an escaped snake in the school.

"The only thing that has escaped is Adam," said Lovely Linda, "from a mad house."

She flashed her teeth in a crushing smile.

Adam didn't even listen. After all he knew the truth. The problem was that he didn't know *where* the truth was. It certainly wasn't hanging from the wall bars any longer.

Adam and his friends set off on a snake hunt. They went through the cloakrooms. They found an old football with no air in it. They found Tracey Grant's lunch box, the one she had lost when she was seven. They also found Lee Carter and Vikki Hugg hiding behind the dustbins. But they didn't find Steak & Kidney.

"What do we do if we *do* see it?" Tracey asked, as they set off to search the playground.

"You call to her. You say 'Here snakey, coochy-coochy, sit, stay ...' What do you think

you do?" grumbled Adam. "You tell me and I'll come and get her."

Mrs Batty watched with interest from the staff room window. Miss Raza stood next to her, sipping her morning coffee.

"That Adam Laker is very strange," she murmured. "I found him on top of the wall bars in the hall this morning."

Mrs Batty's eyebrows shot up her forehead. "Really? That's an odd place to find a toilet. He told me he had to go to the toilet."

The two teachers looked at each other. They gazed back at Adam.

"Strange boy," both said at the same time, shaking their heads.

A moment later their peace and quiet was shattered by a series of screams.

Chapter 6

The Snake Appears at Last

"Aaargh!"

The school caretaker burst onto the playground. He was waving a mop and swinging a toilet brush round and round his head.

"Snake!" screamed the caretaker. "There's a snake in my office!"

In an instant there was panic. Cries of 'Snake! Snake!' filled the air. The smallest children began crying, screaming and running round in circles. Many of the older children thought that was a very good idea too. They started to cry, scream and run round in bigger circles. The caretaker waved his mop and toilet brush.

Teachers came hurrying from all directions. Mr Twigg began questioning the caretaker and almost got hit on the head with the brush. The teachers tried to calm the children and soon they were running round in circles too.

"Are you sure it was a snake?" Mr Twigg asked the caretaker.

The caretaker puffed out his chest – and it was a fat chest.

"It was a snake," he declared. "It was huge. It was a python. I saw one on TV the other night. They can eat whole pigs you know, and goats."

A little five-year-old burst into tears. "Don't let the snake eat my coat," he sobbed. "It's brand new and Mummy said I mustn't lose it. Please don't let the snake eat my coat."

Miss Raza tried to comfort him. She already had seven infants clinging to her legs.

As if there was not enough going on already a new sound made itself heard above the others. It was the sound of a distant siren. Then it became the sound of two sirens, then three, four, five sirens.

The police were on their way to the school. So were the fire brigade. And an ambulance. And the RSPCA. Adam's heart sank into his shoes. He was doomed. There would be no escape for him now.

Police-officers with riot helmets and shields poured into the building. Firemen unrolled great lengths of hose. A young man and woman jumped from their RSPCA van. They took a large, wire cage out of the back. They got out rope and nets. They pulled on thick, leather gloves. They dashed into the school.

A large and excited audience had gathered by the school fence. They were leaning over, trying to see what was going on.

"It's a fire," said an old lady.

"No, no," argued a big-bellied man. "They've all got food poisoning and they're throwing up all over the place."

"That's not what I heard," said a young woman. "I thought the headteacher was crushed by the piano during assembly."

The teachers had managed to gather most of the children together. Now they were standing at the far end of the school field, out of harm's way. Even Adam and his friends had been shuffled onto the grass.

Adam found himself standing next to The Lovely Linda.

"I told you there was a snake," he said.

He was determined to prove his point, even if he was going to end up in massive trouble. Linda pressed her lips together. For once she was silent.

The scene inside the school was frantic. People were running everywhere. Every classroom was being searched. Every office was being inspected. But Steak & Kidney was nowhere to be found.

It was a policeman who found the snake. There she was, coiled up beneath a pile of sacking, in the corner of the caretaker's office. The policeman began to laugh. He carefully picked up the snake in both hands. He marched out to the playground and went straight across to Mr Twigg and the caretaker.

"Is this your snake?" he asked.

The caretaker stared in disbelief at the thick piece of old brown hose draped across the policeman's arms. It was covered with yellow mildew. From a distance it looked just like a python.

The caretaker slowly went redder and redder. He rubbed his bald head. Mr Twigg began to laugh. The teachers laughed. Everyone began laughing. The Lovely Linda turned on Adam.

"I said you never brought a snake to school," she snarled in triumph.

Chapter 7

What Happened in the End?

The playground slowly emptied as people went back to their cars and trucks and ambulances. The crowd drifted away.

The children were lined up in their classes. They filed back into school. Everyone was chattering excitedly but nobody spoke to Adam. His friends had deserted him. They all thought he had tricked them. There had never been a snake at all.

When they got back to class Adam found himself sitting alone. The only person who would look at him was The Lovely Linda. She gave him a mocking smile. Adam hardly noticed. His mind was on another matter. The school had just been searched from top to bottom. So where was Steak & Kidney?

Adam spent the afternoon thinking and thinking. The python must have gone somewhere. Adam sat in his seat and gazed into space. Mrs Batty watched him and shook her head slowly.

"Are you all right, Adam?" she asked.

"What?"

Adam was jerked out of his thoughts. Several children giggled and Mrs Batty sighed.

"You have been behaving very strangely today, Adam. Are you all right? Has all that business with the caretaker upset you?"

Adam stared back at Mrs Batty. The penny dropped. Of course! OF COURSE!!

Adam jumped from his chair and it went tumbling backwards. He raced for the door.

"Where are you going?" cried Mrs Batty.

"Toilet!" yelled Adam and he vanished up the corridor. His teacher sank back into her chair.

"Not up the wall bars, please," she murmured.

Adam raced down the corridor. He skidded round the corner and then slowed down as he reached the caretaker's little room. He stood outside for a moment, getting back his breath. He knocked on the door. There was no reply. Adam edged open the door and peered inside.

"Hello? Anyone in?"

There was still no answer. Adam pushed the door wider and went in.

The room stank of string and socks and polish and bleach. It was a jumble of tins and dusters and brooms. In one corner was the

caretaker's little desk. Five unwashed coffee mugs stood on the table top. Two of them had mould growing in them. The caretaker might clean the school, but he certainly didn't clean his office.

Adam was sure the snake was in that room somewhere. The caretaker really *had* seen the python after all. But when the policeman showed him the old bit of hose he had begun to doubt his own eyes.

Adam pushed aside mountains of tins and cloths. He stood on a chair and examined the shelves. He looked inside the cupboard, and half the contents fell on top of him. There was no sign of Steak & Kidney.

Adam opened the drawer of the desk. Curled up inside, fast asleep, was the python. Adam closed his eyes and gave a thankful prayer. He gathered up the snake. He peered round the door to make sure the coast was clear. Then he

zipped back to the cloakroom to tuck the snake away safely. There were only five minutes to go before home time.

Adam went back to class feeling on top of the world. As he walked in everyone turned to look at him.

"Better?" asked Mrs Batty.

"Brilliant!" grinned Adam. He smiled back at all the faces staring at him. He sat down in his seat and waited for home time.

The bell went and the children headed noisily for the cloakroom. They grabbed their bags and coats and were soon heading for home. The Lovely Linda shook her curls at Adam.

"Some snake," she said.

Adam just shrugged his shoulders and set off for home. He was pretty pleased with the way things had turned out. He hadn't got into trouble after all. He had found Steak & Kidney.

The strangest thing was that even now Adam didn't actually have the python. But at least he knew where the snake was. He had put it in the bottom of The Lovely Linda's bag.

If you loved this,
why don't you try ...

Mad Iris
by Jeremy Strong

Would you like to have an ostrich for a pet? Ross has big problems when one turns up in the school playground. How can he save her from the men in black who want to kill her? And why is Katie stuck in the boys' toilets?

You can order *Mad Iris* directly from our website at www.barringtonstoke.co.uk

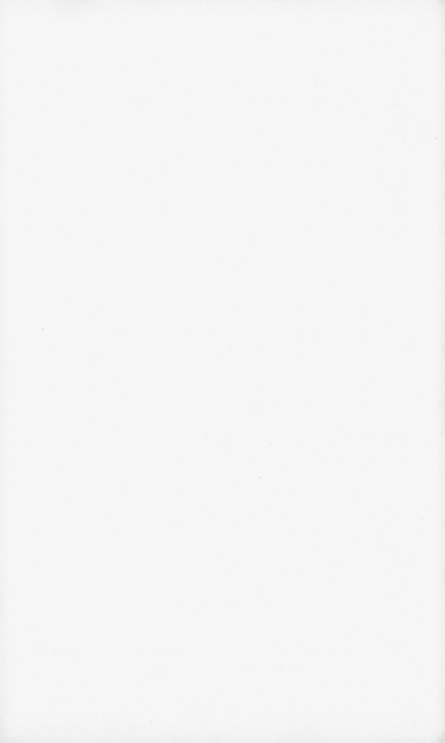